How About A Hug?

by Nancy Carlson

PUFFIN BOOKS

PUFFIN BOOKS
Published by Penguin Group
Penguin Young Readers Group,
345 Hudson Street, New York, New York 10014, U.S.A.
Penguin Books Ltd, 80 Strand, London WC2R ORL, England
Penguin Books Australia Ltd, 250 Camberwell Road, Camberwell, Victoria 3124, Australia
Penguin Books Canada Ltd, 10 Alcorn Avenue, Toronto, Ontario, Canada M4V 3B2
Penguin Books (N.Z.) Ltd, 182-190 Wairau Road, Auckland 10, New Zealand

Penguin Books Ltd, Registered Offices: Harmondsworth, Middlesex, England

First published in the United States of America by Viking,
a division of Penguin Putnam Books for Young Readers, 2001
Published by Puffin Books, a division of Penguin Young Readers Group, 2003

1   3   5   7   9   10   8   6   4   2

THE LIBRARY OF CONGRESS HAS CATALOGED THE VIKING EDITION AS FOLLOWS:
Carlson, Nancy L.
How about a hug? / Nancy Carlson.
p.   cm.
Summary: Questions and answers show the reader that different kinds
of hugs can be the answer for many situations.
ISBN: 0-670-03506-8 (hc)
[1. Hugging—Fiction. 2. Animals—Fiction. 3. Questions and answers.]   I. Title.
PZ7.C21665 Hm 2001 [E]—dc21 2001000510

Puffin Books ISBN 0-14-250144-1

Printed in the United States of America
Set in Clarendon, Life
Book design by Teresa Kielinski

The artwork was created using colored pencil and pen on a hot press paper.

In memory of my uncle Bill,
who always gave me BIG hugs!

It is for cold Monday mornings when you have to get up for school.

It goes really well with pancakes and eggs. What is it?

A Good Morning Hug!

It is for heading off to school

or going to work,

and it helps you feel happy all day. What is it?

A Have a Great Day Hug!

It's for scrapes on knees

and bumps on heads.

It goes well with Band-Aids and suckers. What is it?

An It'll Be A-Okay Hug!

It's for someone you haven't seen in a long time.

It goes well with big chairs

and warm cocoa. What is it?

A Boy Am I Glad to See You Hug!

It's for when you lose the big soccer game

or cross the finish line after everyone else.

It can help you become a better sport. What is it?

A You Did Great Hug!

It's for when you get in a fight with your best friend,

and you miss her a whole lot. What is it?

An I'm Sorry Hug!

It's for scary times,

for meeting new babies,

and for saying good-bye to old friends.

It's for happy times, sad times, kids, and grown-ups,

and it goes well with a kiss. What is it?

It's an Anytime, Anywhere, I Love You Hug!